DIFFERENT STROKES

DIFFERENT STROKES

The Gods are not to blame

By

IKE MORAH

authorHOUSE®

AuthorHouse™
1663 Liberty Drive
Bloomington, IN 47403
www.authorhouse.com
Phone: 1-800-839-8640

First published by AuthorHouse   09/26/2011

ISBN: 978-1-4670-4312-0 (sc)
ISBN: 978-1-4670-4310-6 (ebk)

Library of Congress Control Number: 2011917606

Printed in the United States of America

Any people depicted in stock imagery provided by Thinkstock are models, and such images are being used for illustrative purposes only.
Certain stock imagery © Thinkstock.

This book is printed on acid-free paper.

TABLE OF CONTENTS

INTRODUCTION

In this book, maybe the last in the series to make it a trilogy with the other two, the gods had once more decided to take a closer look at what their supreme creation was up to.

The first in this trilogy was We Us and Others. In it we noticed what the gods did when they all came down to the earth for a festival of the gods. It was claimed to be a festival, not minding the fact that as it had always been with them, the ulterior motive was to observe man. They wanted first class information; at least that was how they put it down in the chronicles of Akpomville, which was a subtitle in the final records of their eonic festival. This was a festival that they organized only once in an eon, though it might look like the twinkle of an eye to them, since they lived a timeless existence. This record was found in the archives of the celestial library. I have not been to this library, but some say that they had been there when they were in the spirit.

God had created man in his own image, we were told. This meant that after man had been molded out of the dust of the earth as it was confirmed by the Christian bible, he breathed into him the breathe of life. This was the spirit that was put into him. It was for this reason that man began to think and eventually acquired the freewill to ask for explanations to issues, demand for his own freedom from whatever, and even challenge the gods as well. As a spirit he was one of them and so he did not seem to know why he should not be able to challenge them.

This acquisition is obvious from certain phrases used during some funeral ceremonies. The most popular is used during the interment, or the commitment of the body to the earth when the official announces: "dust to dust and ash to ash." This is in recognition of the fact that the body had to decay back into the organic earth materials from which it had been molded. The spirit on the other hand takes off to join its other colleagues in the spirit world. In the less civilized societies, these spirits are recognized and often prayed to as ancestral spirits. In the 'civilized world,' where Christianity seems to be the dominant idea, they are recognized and prayed to as saints.

In the second book in the series, Echoes of Yesteryears, Mercury was sent down as a messenger of the gods to come down and find out what was happening. At the end of his visit, mainly to WADICO, he did not see anything to write home about. His opinion seemed to be that there was an ever-growing preponderance of immorality, lawlessness, bribery and corruption and absolute insincerity amongst men. All these were attributed to one of them—Satan. Satan on his part did not quite accept responsibility for that since man had eaten that fruit of knowledge, which gave him the power to know the difference between good and evil. He had made a strong point and they therefore had to accept the fact that it was man that had the power to shape his own future. His fate was in his hands.

As to the ultimate spiritual disposition, which is as to spiritual beliefs and general ideas towards the spirits, all men seem to have the same opinions. This is in relation to religious beliefs. They all seem to look forward towards one great and omnipotent god, no matter what he is called or how he is viewed. The differences are only as to respective perceptions of him, as well as the ways in which he is approached. No matter which road one chose, all the roads seem to lead to the same Supreme Being, irrespective of his name. This could further be viewed from the standpoint of a practical analogy:

We all live in different parts of the earth, but supposing that each person was asked to head for the city of London in Britain, and then we will understand what religious beliefs is all about. London to some could be a respectable city, to some it could be an irrelevant city and to others yet it could be their capital and so on. Those living in the west will go east to get there, just as those in the east will go west. Those in the north will go south and those in the south will go north. This will also apply to the various other cardinal points. Many will go by private cars, some by public transportation. Many will go by sea and others yet by air. Do not forget that there are still those who will go on foot. Amongst those on foot some will walk, some will jog and yet others will run. There will be many ways to get there but the main thing is that all are heading there.

All said and done, this means that there are different ways and means to the same end. For this reason it might seem as if we are all geared towards the same religious end. It is the perception and ways of practice that differ. One might call him God, another Allah. Some might call him Yahweh and others Chineke and yet there are those who might look upon him as the universal force or even simply as nature. Be that which it may, it is all the same God. It is the human intolerance and lack of understanding that leads to misunderstandings and even wars.

No matter how one looks at it, in this book, it was that very supreme being who had called on the other spiritual beings, for there are many of them otherwise he would not be supreme, to arrange to send emissaries back to earth to see what man had deteriorated to. He was of the opinion that man was now in an age that could very easily be looked on as 'the age of decadence.' Man had now challenged the gods and he was well on the path of power acquisition and dominion over others.

DIFFERENT STROKES

As to how and why particular spirits were chosen for these missions we do not know, but the important thing to note is that many groups were sent down to earth. The first to arrive was the group led by Agaba-Idu. This was a very fierce looking ancestral spirit. He was very powerful, and everyone feared him. Humans will all run for safety at the mere sight of him while even some of the other spirits would prefer to keep a respectable distance from him. He was the spirit who sort of personified the devil, if not in deeds then at least in looks. He was claimed not to be as wicked as he looked.

He had a hideous and heinous looking human face with oversized teeth. Just that sight of this face alone could send many Lilly-livered humans into instant convulsions. His eyes were very large and wide and they also protruded way out of the rest of the face. The locks of his hair were even more dreadful. They came down in indeterminate coiffeurs. Some of the strands were snakes, just like as with Medusa who tackled with the Argonaughts, but these were not real snakes. Some of the strands could be seen clutching dead chickens and vultures. His general stance was that of an evil domineering spirit come down to chastise man.

He often carried a sword or machete in one hand, and in this era of terrorism he could even carry a gun. Once in a while he could be seen with his twin brother—Ngbadike. They were not identical twins, but the looks were close enough. According to the archives of the celestial birth registry, it was claimed that their mother—Ajambene—after she had broken a rotten coconut. She had smashed it on the ground and it split into two unequal halves. One turned into Agaba—Idu and the other into Ngbadike. They were miniatures of their current selves. The miracle there was that they each sprang into her womb and that was the beginning of a five-year gestational period before they were finally given birth to.

They were not particularly close to each other. Ngbadike did not see why his brother should be regarded as senior to him when they emerged from the coconut at the same time. He therefore always tried to pursue him. This was why, whenever he came out, a rope was tied around his waist and one human or the other was allowed to hold onto the rope to restrain him from going after his brother. Once in a while he would turn around and go after this restrainer. It always reminded one of a version of the biblical account of Cain and Abel revisited, though those two were not twins. The roles however seem reversed this time around. Here it is the younger one that wanted the recognition.

When this special emissary came down he knew exactly what to expect. He had an idea of what was going on amongst the humans because their natural inclination was towards the survival of the fittest and the domination of the weak by the more powerful. He was not totally unfamiliar with that trend where the more powerful villages tried to lord it over the weaker ones. They were simply being colonized. He was familiar with this situation because he was one of the fighters who had joined Lucifer to revolt against God in the heavens, according to the Christian accounts.

There would be no need to discuss how he got to earth or how long it took him. In the spiritual realm, a thousand years would seem simply like the twinkle of an eye and so it might suffice to say that he simply arrived with his brother and a few others. He was the leader of the delegation. In The Echoes of Yesteryears we saw the villages, but now many of them had changed. He was headed for Acadia, but he found himself in Utopia. Utopia was a much smaller village than Acadia and it was also very much weaker, but it was, by all accounts, a very complex society and that reminded him of the biblical account of what had happened to man earlier on. According to the bible:

> "... and the whole earth was of one language and one speech."

> (Genesis Ch 11, Vs 1)

It was for this reason that they were able to conspire and attempt to build the tower of Babel under the guidance of Nimrod the great hunter. They were the descendants of Noah after the flood that wiped out the entire earth. Because god knew what was in their heart; he realized that nothing could stop them from achieving their imaginations. They would have probably, and the likelihood of that was great, used it to climb into heaven and see what god was doing there and maybe try to overthrow him. It was for this reason that he took action right away:

> "Go to, let us go down, and there confound their language,
> that they may not understand one another's speech."

> (Genesis Ch 11, Vs 7)

This was exactly the situation in Utopia. Geographically, Utopia was situated in an area that stretched from the mangrove forests of the great ocean to the semiarid regions of the great desert. Every imaginable climate was in effect there due to the fact that it could be very hot since they were not too far from the equator and it could be cold and snowy in the higher elevations of their mountain ranges. Linguistically they spoke it near to an innumerable number of mutually unintelligible languages and dialects. In short they could not understand each other.

To make matters worse, their customs were as diverse as their languages. Some would, for instance, practice the matrilineal system of inheritance while to others it was patrileneal. Some were therefore highly machoistic societies whereas others were purely feministic in outlook. In some the soldiers were only men and in others they were mixed while yet in a few they were amazons.

There were many tribes and clans here. In some, councils of elders ruled them, like in WADICO—fear God honor the king—in the Echoes of yesteryears, but kings ruled others. Queens ruled many of them and just chiefs ruled others. Whilst those who had kings prided themselves at paying homage to their rulers others prided themselves at not having anyone to obey.

There were tribes that existed within strict moral codes, and yet there were others where immorality was held in high esteem even if not openly. It was amongst this set that the visitors got confused about. They claimed to have strict moral codes and yet when they were asked to preach abstinence from sex early on in life, they preferred to provide condoms instead. It was therefore obvious that to them, fornication was nothing, and anyway later on in life adultery had to be the norm for married couples who often found it very hard to keep to within themselves alone.

Still on the differences, many of these tribes were physically totally different from each other, and when it came to religious beliefs confusion was the case. Though externally different, they were the same internally, even when it came to beliefs in general. Even amongst the Christians it was the same just as they had pointed out in the bible:

> "And there are differences in administration, but the same Lord. And there are diversities of operations but it is the same God which worketh all in all."

> (1 Corinthians Ch. 12, Vs 5 & 6)

This would seem further correct when we consider their behaviors and religious inclinations and it looks funny when viewed from this angle.

There were the Naturalists who believed in the natural order of things and that it was nature that controlled everything. To them, every power was already innate in man and not acquired. All the powers were normal and a consequence of nature, which in their own case was therefore supreme.

There were the atheists who believe that there was no god. They however believe that there was a supreme hand that controlled all events. What this supreme hand was did not seem to matter to them. It will therefore not be out of place for one to imagine that they did not believe in a supreme being and yet they are aware of the fact that there is an inexplicable order of things—obviously controlled by a supreme hand of fate.

The mystics on their part believe that there is a supreme being be it god or nature or even hand, and that one could also be able to attain mastership and be able to commune with and also be one with it. In other words, theirs was the belief in the possibility of one attaining direct communion with god together with the acquisition of the knowledge of spiritual truths, often through meditations. It is not just this acquisition of knowledge that is involved but also that of power too.

All the aforementioned make up only about ten percent minority amongst religious believers. The bulk of the village was claimed to be made up of those who claimed to be monotheists—that is those who believed in the existence of one Supreme Being, despite their belief in many others for that is the basis of that one being supreme. They make up the remaining ninety percent of the population, but the real issue is that they were actually what one of them referred to as whatever believers. They went to their respective religious houses regularly, but they are predominantly oblivious of their religious teachings. Only a miserable three percent of these practiced what their religious sects taught. Even the priests were as non-compliant as the masses that they led. That is surely an instance of the blind leading the blind masses.

It was therefore less than three percent of the entire population that practiced what they preached. Agaba was convinced that this was a country of nonbelievers when one went to the realities of the case. Be that as it may, they were at each other's throats.

It was while they were bickering amongst each other that Acadia struck. They came in by force and cunning and in no time at all they had taken over Utopia.

With a couple of DIFFERENT STROKES, each arbitrarily made, Acadia carved out towns as well as villages by creating boundaries that were oblivious of all those differences. Previous towns, tribes and even kingdoms were lumped together and amalgamated, as it was called. Acadia had become an imperial power. She had created an empire by forming different colonies, which she administered solely for commercial interests. These states were ruled by Acadia and eventually many of them were granted freedom to rule themselves, as if they did not rule themselves before the interference.

Might is power, for that was the rule of the survival of the fittest. Acadia had become a colonial master and Utopia had become one of her colonies. She had been created out of different arbitrary strokes on a map. When Acadia was questioned as to why she had to do that, all she did was to quote a portion from that Christian bible:

> "Behold, how good and how proper it is for brethren to dwell together in unity!"
>
> (Psalm Ch 135, Vs 4)

What they did not have in common did not matter; all that mattered was that they had to exist together, even if as a patchwork of incorporated tribes and clans. Acadia had however tried to modernize Utopia though this was done with part of the loot that they had derived from there. Roads were built and schools were erected. More modern ways of life were introduced and these included the shedding of the idea of extended family ties and obligations. The society was expected to move more towards absolute individualism where the norm was every man for himself, and maybe the gods for all. One was no longer expected to be his brother's keeper.

Chiefs, kings and kingdoms were done away with, while democracy took root together with its ability to attract certain ills—bribery and corruption, together with deceit and the overpowering urge to grasp power. Freedom of speech and actions had come in while lying had become normal and acceptable.

The rights of individuals to various issues had been introduced, including the right for one to behave as he willed. When it came to religion, it was promptly supported by the state though simply relegated to the background as they tried to keep it apart from governance.

Religious principles were so relegated to the background that the state was free to abuse its basic principles. For instance though Utopia was a predominantly Christian nation, the state did not only encourage but also advertised the idea of the freedom for one to marry whomever he willed. Though the bible was strictly against a man getting married to another man or a woman doing the same, they simply encouraged it. In fact there was that group that advocated that the government should respect and support their idea that humans had the right to marry their pets. It was not acceptable, but then, the government did not discourage the idea. They were simply quiet over that and for many; silence was another way of indicating support.

The gods did not seem to be particularly happy with this development. Agaba Idu did not continue to Acadia since he had seen that it had domineered Utopia to such an extent that it had become a mirror image of Acadia itself.

He simply asked members of his group that they should go back; otherwise they might come across things that might make them try to destroy man. Their mission was to find out whether man was still all out to acquire power and domineer others. They had seen it first hand but they did not continue to find out what was happening when she decided to fight anyone that tried to resist it since that portion belonged to another group.

They therefore went back and filed their reports, which were not encouraging in any way whatsoever.

THE GAMES

The next group of emissaries to leave the heavens was the group that was charged with the job of confirming what they already knew, that man can never be trusted even when he is entertaining himself.

Ulo, who was the patron saint of sportsmen and the very same god who, it was rumored, helped Achilles with his athletic prowess, was their leader. He was however known to have once interfered in a soccer match, but such interferences were only acceptable and a prerogative of the gods. His favorite team was about to loose a match when he magically got the opposing goalkeeper to kick the ball into his own net. It was claimed to have been a botched attempt at passing the ball to his back man who was watching his back when there was no scramble at the goalmouth. Even he himself was not too sure of how he had achieved that feat. An own goal was not exactly unknown, though very uncommon, but this one was bizarre in all aspects of it since the back man was not actually behind him as he had claimed.

Ulo was not the regular type of spirit and he was largely invisible to humans, though he could manifest in any form whenever he wished. Many other members of his contingent were however ancestral spirits and people were used to them. Osondu was the demigod of athletes. Whenever he wanted an athlete to perform better he would manifest himself behind the athlete and remain visible only to him. He would be there pursuing him as a cheetah and the person would run for his life and so perform better. It was under such a condition that one of the Olympic athletes set an unbreakable record.

Dingba was the patron saint of wrestlers. He was assisted in this by his half brother, Headlock, after whom the triple headlock maneuver was named. Akataka was also one of them. He was the playful ancestral spirit that was in the habit of chasing young boys around during festivals. His closest friend was Eyo, who was another playful spirit.

They had all set off for Acadia. Acadia was their choice because there was an international tournament going on there. It was a soccer tournament and it was the world cup finals. Their main mission was to see how humans behaved during sports events. It is not that they did not already know what was already happening for they are omniscient, but there was nothing like having a first hand information and experience.

They arrived just as the tournament began but they stayed there incognito as spirits, remaining invisible since there were no vacant seats left in the stadium. They hung around the Very Important Personality zone when the first match started. It was between WADICO and WADICO—fear God honor the king. These were two different villages. It was a game, and as with all games there was going to be a winner and a looser. It was a game quite all right, but one should also not forget that these were two warring villages that had been at each other's throat for some time now. This war had however been introduced into the soccer field and the game had turned into a do or die affair.

During the early minutes of the game, one player pointed out to his opponent that he dribbled the ball like a sissy. His opponent replied with a devastating head butt to his face. That drew a lot of blood from his nostrils. The referee halted the match for a while during which time he gave a red card to the man who had executed that effective head butt. He also allowed the other team to replace the wounded player without the replacement counting towards the allowable maximum number of replacements allowed in a game.

That was not however the end of the matter. The player that was given the red card had been ejected and so he could not be replaced. The other team was not going to let that happen—to continue with one player short. As their opponent's captain came to save a ball during a goalmouth scramble, they floored him. He had received a vicious kick to his knee and that was enough to break his kneecap. The match was once more stopped, the captain carried out on a stretcher, the kicker given just a yellow card and then a penalty awarded to their opponent. The referee had come to the conclusion that a yellow card together with a penalty kick was enough punishment. Apart from that, another red card might help reduce the number of players in the field to ten apiece.

The crowd went wild with cheering for excellent officiating but that suddenly gave way to silence as the goalkeeper miraculously caught the goal bound ball. A couple of the celestial emissaries immediately began to suspect that Ulo must have interfered, but they were wrong. Be that as it may, the match had to continue and at the end it was a drawn game. The two sworn enemies left the field feeling more bitter against each other more than before.

In the match that followed this one a queer situation came to light. By the time that the match officially ended, it was a goalless draw since the two sides were equally matched. However, during the last ten seconds of the injury time the left full back of one of the teams attempted a failed bicycle kick. Well, it would be a failed kick depending on who is thinking of it. It had come from a spectacular acrobatic maneuver, but his instep did not connect properly and so quite unfortunately he only managed to send the ball past his own goalkeeper for an own goal. It was the only goal of the match and he had simply handed a win over to his opponents. He immediately fell to the ground and began to cry uncontrollably, but that was not the main issue.

As soon as they got home from the tournament, a chain of events was set in motion. To start with, he was expelled from the team. The president of his country declared a day of mourning for a loss to their rabid enemy. He finally sent the expelled player into a self-imposed exile. That was not all. On his way out of the country, a 'stray' bullet from a law enforcement officer's rifle hit him, after an accidental discharge. He died from that bullet wound.

The match the following day was between another two sworn enemies. Newt had beaten their opponent Salamander and within twenty-four hours of the match the two countries went into a full-scale war. This war was recorded as the three-day war that was precipitated by sports fanaticism. Close to five thousand lives were lost in this war.

Many other queer things happened during this match, a few of which were attributed to the presence of these gods. Mind you, interference by the gods in matches is not abnormal and that was how they managed to come up with the saying: "the gods of soccer were not on their side." How true that saying could be. That was however wrong for they were there as impartial observers. At one stage for instance, an attacker had tried to kick home an already goal bound ball. The ball would have probably gone into the net but he tried to make assurance double sure by aiming for the side from where the goalkeeper had just moved. Instead the ball hit the referee on the back and only managed to slip in by the goalkeeper.

It was definitely a goal, but according to the other side the referee was not authorized to score for either side. The referee insisted that he did not score the goal since the ball was already goal bound. The team that had the advantage however had a totally different view of the matter. First of all a goal was a goal and technically speaking, they had scored a goal. However they accused the referee of trying to help the other side. According to them, the ball would have gone into the net at the end from where the goalkeeper had moved but instead it just managed to slip through his hands at the other end after he had tried to make sure that it did not enter the net. Fortunately for them, "the gods of soccer were still on their side."

The football association was divided on their opinions about this issue. There had never been a precedent to draw from. The emissaries were also divided on the issue. It was therefore obvious that when it came to the affairs of man, complications and confusions were the norm, especially regarding games.

As for the countries from which the two teams had come, their reaction was simple, swift and expected. They immediately mutually recalled their ambassadors.

When the tournament got to the semifinal stage, the emissaries were in for a totally new twist in the affairs of man. Bribery and corruption had come to be factored into the equation. The very first match had been fixed. It was a match between the number one ranked team and the tournament surprise—the team that was ranked number thirty-eight. It was a team that managed its way to the semifinals by a series of defaults. Some of her opponents had withdrawn and two were disqualified, each just before a match. The match was being played at home which meant that they were Acadians. They had therefore drawn bye at various stages. In their quarterfinal match, the opposing team went on strike just after the starting whistle. It was a strike against their countries' sports organizing body. A group of interested parties had put this idea into their heads, all with a little monetary support.

They had refused to play till the referee pointed it out to them that they could all be punished individually for that and so they started to play. They refused to score any goal till towards the end of the goalless display before they dribbled backwards and sent the ball sizzling into their own net. Of course their village lost the match and their organizing body got the message though it was already too late for any meaningful amends.

This could only be rivaled by what took place during one of the earlier matches. In this particular case the match started just as one of the religious groups was about to start their prayers. One of the goalkeepers happened to belong to that group. Just as he knelt down for a very short prayer, he saw the ball sail harmlessly into his net. It was within four seconds of the start of the match. This was possible and so fast because they were trying out a new strategy. As soon as they passed the ball, the center forward had sent it backwards to the full back, who promptly passed it on to the praying goalkeeper. The idea was to draw their opponents out of their goalmouth area as early as possible. It had only misfired.

To make matters worse, the second goal had come in quick succession to the first. Members of his team were still in a bad mood from the first goal and he was still trying to come into grips with the situation, when the ball once more came sizzling home. By the time the first half ended, the team was as good as useless and hopeless. It was the eleventh goal that found its way into the net—one for each player in the field—when the referee ended the first half. In this particular case, he had expected the back man to head the ball away, but the back man was only trying to deceive their opponents so that he could catch the ball. Each of them had dodged the ball.

The president of their country had called and disbanded the team even before they could come out for the second half. In reply the sports governing body immediately banned the country from participating in any of their tournaments for three years.

Back to the Acadians; they had miraculously won the semifinal match and were bound for the finals. Of course the gods were all—knowing and they knew what had actually happened. The stronger team had been paid off by the mafia to loose. Betters knew that the number one ranked club was going to win and they had all betted heavily on them. Not only were they paid for this; most of their families were kidnapped and held hostage till the end of the match. Of course everyone lost his bet, except for those who ran the number games.

The issue of sports had become so emotionally charged that many sports commissions were dismantled without notice for loosing games. They had introduced replay of scenes from the matches so that referee decisions could be challenged and if possible changed. This was to be based on fairness. Players were bribed to loose matches and referees were paid to influence the outcome of matches. All these helped to change the games from what they were meant to be, into something else. They were initially institutes purely for entertainment and both the loosers and the winners always celebrated. That time was gone and there was nothing that the gods could do about that except to note that man was getting too greedy. The unbridled urge to acquire wealth, fame and power had taken over.

ALCOHOL

Thus far the reports had not been very encouraging, and so the third group was sent out. This was the group that was supposed to investigate into what man did for recreation, especially when it came to the use of alcohol. Bacchus was asked to head this group. They were to concentrate on hotels, casinos and drinking bars.

Bacchus was the chairman of the group, with Iti as his co-chairman. It was suspected that any of them could get drunk and that was why it was necessary for this group to have a co-chairman. The member whom no one seemed to be sure of whom she was seemed to be Jolly, the goddess of jollity, as it was put. Aphrodite, the goddess of beauty was with them as well as Akalogoli, the demigod and patron saint of all the irresponsible drunks. It was because of this last member that most drunks always managed to get home in one piece even while being out of their minds.

When they manifested themselves, it was at the Bromocarbadi Hotel in Utopia. It was Akalogoli who chose this particular hotel for them. His reason was that it represented the rest very well in all imaginable areas. Who else would know better when it came to such issues? It was actually Ajondu, the junior brother to Akalogoli, who coined the name of that hotel. He had made up that name from the words: BROthel, Motel, CAsino, BAR and Diner. He was a frequent visitor to that hotel and he delighted in protecting those who lived a reckless life too.

On manifestation, they found themselves in the lobby of this five star hotel. It was a cozy place, it was a comfortable place and it was like paradise on earth. It is claimed that all that glitters is not gold and that was what they found out later. As innocent as the entire place looked, it was the grand headquarters and den of iniquity. It was the bastion of human immorality and a direct product of civilization and modernization, which could be seen as an attempt by man to head towards his own destruction.

Their first experience of this was when they asked to be taken to the rooms that had been reserved for them, so that they could freshen up. Each of them was ushered into his room by a girl and each of theses girls could well go for a beauty queen. Many of them were actually a match for Aphrodite, who was amongst them.

When Bacchus got to his room, the usher offered to help undress him. He found that very embarrassing and quickly declined the offer. She then offered to help him out with a hot bath and that was even worse. What the girl did not know was that he was just a spirit that had just manifested into human form. She finally offered to get him some drinks, and that was of course one offer that Bacchus could never refuse. He however nearly jumped out of his earthly skin when she came in with the drinks. She had wheeled in the drink cart completely naked! She was totally nude. Bacchus was a mature and relatively disciplined god and so he managed to ask her to come back in about an hour's time. That was how he managed to get rid of her. On her way out she also managed to remind him that she was there to help him and was ready to provide him with whatever he wanted, with an emphasis on the word 'whatever,' as well as a mischievous wink.

He knew exactly what she meant and he only nodded. He knew that they were all there to entertain the guests and make some money. They were prostitutes, or preferably escorts, which is the name by which they are known nowadays.

As for Aphrodite, they had provided a male usher for her. In her own case the man fell down in a swoon as he beheld her beauty, and so he was immediately replaced with a lesbian usher. Aphrodite found that to be an insult since she was in the habit of taunting her beauty before the male gods. She therefore asked that she should not be provided with an usher.

Iti had a similar experience as Bacchus, but in his own case, he managed to preach to the girl. He tried to convince her to mend her ways lest she found herself in hell at the end. Those words of course fell on deaf ears. Jolly did not however send off her own usher without giving her a few passionate, and according to him, hot kisses.

Lest I forget, it was claimed that when it came to Akalogoli, he surprised the rest of them. He did not do what they had expected him to do. He simply took pity on the girl and then gave her a lot of money and asked her to go home and not to sin any more.

Having rested for a while, they all decided to go down to the dancing hall for a little exercise. What they saw was not what they had expected. Most of the people were seated on one side watching topless and often nude girls dancing on a stage. Those sitting on the other side were watching male dancers on another stage. Each side attracted a mixed clientele. From each side they made provocative and suggestive moves and the spectators cheered wildly. As for the gods, they found all that nauseating at the least. To them, what was the point in removing their clothes to dance if not that they wanted to be more like the wild animals. This suggested to them that the society was into certain decadence.

They were convinced that this was the adult section of the dancing floor and so they sneaked in to the main floor. Here two life bands were performing on the same stage, but they alternated. When one of them played it's music, the people danced wildly, but it was their dance moves that they found annoying. The latest move in town was for each dancer to make moves that would look as provocatively sexy as possible. In other words it was more of a sex dance than any other thing and that came to prove that man had gone so far down as to make sex their main attraction.

When the second band took over it was a totally different story. It looked as if the sexy dances had only put them on. The beats, and so the steps, were deliberately mild and slow while the overall music was excitingly mesmerizing. Partners held tight to each other with some hardly moving. Some were kissing and a few were fumbling and those were all in the name of dancing. They were sure that right in the middle some would actually be busy doing their own things.

They were already disgusted when they left the dancing floor and headed for the casino area. The casino was in the next building and so they had to take a dimly lit alley to the place. What they saw could best be described as something else. Couples were everywhere making out against the walls, and barely ten yards from there was the nude beach area that they had created. Everyone there was completely nude as they milled around 'in a civilized manner.'

It so happened that all the gods were already blushing by the time they got to the casino building. The story was however slightly different inside there. People were busy playing at all sorts of games. There were many card as well as dice games, but people seemed to troop more towards the slot machines. Of course it did not escape them as they noticed that the dice were loaded just as the cards were magical and the slot machines set to spit out winnings very often, though what came out was a miserly twenty percent of what went in.

To make people have a more cheerful disposition and dig deeper into their pockets, drinks were served free at intervals. As they found out however, the beer was laced with vodka while the soft drinks had their fair share of the same. Bacchus and company were therefore very much at home there. Each of them had been claimed to be able to turn water into wine and vice versa. Aphrodite went about doing what she did best—taunting both the men and the lesbians. Even some gay men began to nurture the idea of a change of mind.

At one stage, Bacchus was so drunk that he jumped onto the dice table and began to dance. He was however a god and so when he realized that he was drunk, he quickly got the alcohol out of his system and in the twinkle of an eye he was once more sober. Though they were there to investigate, their charge was that they should mingle to find out every thing. Akalogoli simply mingled. He was a very irresponsible god and he was in his milieu. He had conjured up a couple of chips and so he was busy gambling with them. He had also chatted up a couple of chicks in the process and in no time at all he had become the hottest gentleman on the floor.

They were each almost drunk, well just as drunk as gods could get, when Iti found out why there were so many doors around there. Each door led into a room that the gamblers used for strictly immoral endeavors. Akalogoli on learning of that quickly checked out three of the rooms in quick succession with three different girls. It could be a casino, but it was technically a motel and functionally a brothel in disguise. Most of the girls lived in those rooms and they were there for rent to their clients for those immoral indiscretions. They could no longer beer it and so they left for the nearby film house.

They were already at the Predator, the film house, before they found out that it was an x-rated adult film that was being shown. A couple of nine-year olds were there, arguably being guided by their parents through the film. That was the basis of the PG (parent guidance) system of film rating. This was a system that was invented in order to let people retain their right to the freedom of expression, no matter how obnoxious the expression might be. It also made sure that parents had the right to choose what their kids were to watch. According to one parent who came with his six-year old daughter: "she will learn about these things sooner or later and so why not sooner?" This was definitely an introduction from the former colonizers of Utopia in an attempt to modernize and get them to be more civilized.

As nauseating as things might have been so far, they were in for the ultimate shock when they visited a small school there. One might ask what their mission had to do with a school, but the reason is that gamblers used to leave their children there while going into the casino next door. These were mainly innocent eleven-year olds and a few others around that age.

They all wore high boots, skimpy half blouses with very low necklines to expose a little bit below the little cleavage that they might have. Their skirts were even more problematic. They were in the ultra mini category. Most of their skirts were only marginally shorter than their underwears. In short, they were each as good as naked in their classrooms as they eagerly taunted whatever small goods they had. The oldest amongst them, a twelve-year old was even bold enough to make advances at Akalogoli who only managed to resist.

One disturbing fact that they found out was what they did not notice inside the hotel—drugs. The hotel had been so smart that visitors will never know that there were drug users there. Their drug zone, as they learnt later was the basement of the building. There, drug dealers sold any drugs of addiction that one wanted to him, and one could relax there and use it. People smoked pot, inhaled cocaine and methamphetamine and injected heroin. It was all as good as legal in the basement. In the school however, the girls did these things openly in the class. One may find it hard to believe this, but if the teacher asked any of them a question that she did not know, all she had to do would be to offer him a bit of her drugs in exchange for the answer.

They had seen all that they wanted to see and so they headed for the diner on their way home. Ambrosia of the gods was their normal food and so nothing in the diner attracted them. They sold a lot of oversized portions of unhealthy foods that were full of fats. Apart from that, they were surprised to find out that their most favorite food was a delicacy made from crabs. Why crabs? They are the loneliest and lowliest of all animals. Why not vultures instead of the crabs. These were the scavengers of the sea. Just as if that was not enough, the chefs special for the day was roach kebab. It consisted of cockroaches strung up on spits with onions and tomatoes before roasting. In other words they ate whatever came their way since God had commanded them to eat all. This was the only commandment from the bible that they were able to obey.

As for this mission and its members: they had come, they had seen and they had run home.

FESTIVAL

It was harvest time and the gods had decided to send the next set of emissaries down to earth. We had come across Akpomville in the first book in this series, We Us and Others, and now the natives were just beginning to harvest their farm products. It was therefore time for their Ifejioku festival. This was a traditional festival, but then it was so organized that it was also time for the Christian harvest and bazaar events both of which complimented each other. Trees and hedges were pruned in this village, which in the new dispensation, happens to be the provincial capital of Utopia. All the trimmed trees, as well as houses were already decorated with multicolored lights.

Most people had been saving all year long to have enough money to spend during this period. The children were all agog with expectations and almost all have had new haircuts for the occasion. Many of them had earned new clothes depending on how well they had behaved during the year. As for the damsels, they were all busy putting finishing touches to their most precious possession—their hairs. Incidentally it was during such a festival in times gone by that one of them asked her fiancée to cut off her head and carry it in his bag so that the rains would not damage her hairdo. To her, her hair was more important than her life. The idiot of a husband obliged her. He did not only live to regret that action which he had taken just to please her but he was in total agony having been imprisoned for life on murder charges.

Tangled hairs were straightened and some were colored in various colors. Most however had their hairs braided, usually with additional attachments. These braids therefore came down in all sorts of coiffeurs and thicknesses as well as in various hues and lengths. Their hairs were actually the crown jewels of their existence.

Many ancestral spirits were also gearing up for brief appearances during these festivals. Most of the men, unlike Cain in the bible, were busy choosing the best from their harvests for the occasion. These were going to be offered to the celestial beings one way or the other.

Ifejioku, the god after whom this festival was named was the leader of the contingent, while Ani, the mother goddess of the earth was there as the supervisor. She was the ultimate female goddess and also in charge of the fertility portfolio. It was because of her that the farmers had come into a season of unprecedented bountiful harvest. Banza, the god of bazaars was also with them and he was the most eager of the entire lot. It was a fairly small though powerful contingent and they materialized in Akpomville, which was not altogether unfamiliar to them, for the festivals.

Though most of the indigenes of this village were Christians, they had not forgotten their roots, and so these two festivals were combined into one compound celebration. It was a four-day event. The first two days were devoted to the Christian portion of the celebrations; the first to the harvest and thanksgiving and the second to the bazaar itself. The final two days, which often tend to be more interesting, were devoted to the traditional celebrations of the same thanksgiving. Why two different celebrations? These people loved to celebrate. In fact, they so loved festivals and celebrations that they even had a festival in remembrance of a previous festival

Their initial materialization was at the Saint Bottles Church of Bacchus. Many had argued that this was not a Christian church, but believe it or not, their pastor was a fully ordained Roman Catholic priest, even if he had been defrocked, but he was not. This was in an era when Roman Catholic priests were still allowed to marry and their nuns known to have children, even if they were no longer alive. In fact, according to Akawo, the celestial documentarian, it was during this period when the Saint Bottles church was formed that celibacy was fully enforced. According to the records, many of the nuns had children for the priests and these children were often killed. What an irony and unfairness. The new priests were forced to be celibate and the nuns were allowed to marry—to their Lord. The problem was that of fornication and adultery.

The priests had their way with the nuns and to them it was fornication; while the nuns had their way with the priests and that was adultery since they were married. In Utopia they fought for the freedom of fair treatment, for why should the women be allowed to be married but not the men? It was also at this stage that a protesting priest revolted. He divorced his wife and went to live with another man. To make matters worse, he was promoted for that and made a Bishop not long after that, he got married to his partner and they wedded in his church. Initially the gods saw this as a slap in the face, but that was the lot of man—to challenge the gods and opt for hell. It was their right to do so.

It was amidst all this confusion that the priest at Saint Bottle's church opted out too. He was fighting, first amongst other reasons, for the freedom of a church to choose and have its own saint. They finally changed the mode of the Eucharist and the church was born.

According to this sect of Christians, the mother church used wine derived from grapes for their Eucharist mainly because that was the only type of wine available in the area where they originated. As for themselves they wanted to be fair. There were now different wines in different areas of the world and so any of them was fair game, especially now that Christianity had gone international. Whichever was the local wine where they lived became the wine of choice for this rite. For this particular church therefore it came to be the palm wine of which Itikili, the identical twin brother of Iti was the inventor. It was that milky sweet juice from different parts of the oil palm tree.

The next wine of choice was the Odeku, which was a devilishly dark brew that was often marketed as liquid food. It was claimed to contain all sorts of secret nourishments that the body might require. This was the big bottle of this Irish brew. When properly aged, it was often given to blood donors so that their recovery might get faster. Whether this actually worked or not is not an issue now. What matters is that it was being done, at least in good fate.

They were there just in time to see and hear the adherents witness to Bacchus. For the host the priest had given them each a large bolus of 'akpu', which was pounded tapioca that had been fully coated with ewedu soup for easy passage through the throat. "This is my body," he intoned as he handed each adherent one lump of this foofoo. This was swallowed with relish and then quickly followed by a generous amount of palm wine. to wash it down. For this second part, he would intone: "This is my blood." The main difference between them and the mother church is that people were now free to administer this sacrament to themselves all day long. For this reason most of them will go home happy and drunk. To them they were not exactly drunk. They were only in close communion with the spirits, though they were mainly with those other spirits that dwelt within the potent wine bottles and jars.

It should be noted that most of them were not exactly interested in those rites, during this festival period. They were thinking of the harvests and the bazaars. It is for this reason that it would not be necessary to go into the rites or even the sermons. The only noteworthy fact was that the power did mention that man had gone too far towards the acquisition of money.

Though he had pointed out that he was not rich and that god was not a god for the rich alone, did not fail to point out that he was not interested in money as such. He however also pointed out that he was a god of all possibilities and for their own sake it would help if each person could reach as far down into his pocket as he could to make donations to the church. He did not fail to remind them that one could never reap where he did not sow and also that one could only reap as much as he had sown. "Sow very healthy seeds and a bountiful harvest will follow." That was vintage evangelical preaching in Utopia. According to him, it therefore followed that the more one gave the more he would reap. Give more to the Lord and you will receive the most powerful prayer of your lives he also reminded them.

To show that he was very modern and current he went on to compare that with the investment environment. He had assured them that the more one invested in good stocks then the more the returns on his investments would be. Many members of the congregation were businessmen and he was appealing to them. They could understand what he was saying and so they donated more than they had intended to. He went on to explain to them that in the case of the parable about the widow's mite in the bible, she had given all that she had. He was not going to encourage them to give all they had, but then it would be worth their while if they donated as much of that as they could.

At the end of the service there was a deafening AMEN! Everyone was waiting for it all to end so that they could go out and see what items had been donated. It was going to be great since the harvest was the most bountiful in recent memory. Akpomville was a farming based provincial headquarters. Many had given the best they had just like the biblical Abel, but a few had actually given next to nothing. Some of these were those who believed that any donations to the church were going to be mismanaged. If members of the committee did not steal most of it, then the priest will make sure that some would find their ways out of the church coffers. That was the way of individually administered churches. Some of these people had actually only presented the discards from their harvests.

It was time for the auctions and they watched the auctioneer, a sharp-tongued schemer, weave his way through the bids. He sold an immensely large turkey for what should be about ten times its fair market price. It was a tug of war between two of their most illustrious sons, before one of them eventually bought it.

An old lady had donated a very large apple, which grew, behind her house. It looked very large and appetizing and the auctioneer was a match for the bidders. It was going to be the star item for the day. He had delayed its sale because they were waiting for the chief to arrive. To make the apple more worthy of a good price the auctioneer told it's history. According to him, it grew on a young tree and it was the first time the tree produced. Furthermore it was the only fruit that it bore. Whoever bought it was going to be blessed and the chief was going to pray over it at the end. A businessman finally bought it. All said and done, this fruit that would probably go for about fifty cents in the market, went for a staggering one thousand dollars.

He promptly paid for it, inspected it, and then gallantly handed it back to the auctioneer to be resold. A deafening applause followed this gesture. It was eventually bought once more, but this time around, it was for fifty dollars. It was handed over to the chief who happily prayed over it, offered it to the spirits who of course did not eat material things. He therefore got his aide to slice it into tiny bits, which were passed round to people. Everyone struggled for a piece of this.

The emissaries did not fail to notice and appreciate how the person who was to give the prayers over the apple was chosen. Initially it was presented to the first man who bought it, but he declined on the grounds that he was not all that worthy of the gods, moreover his father was there, which only meant that he felt that he was too young to be given that honor. In some communities, but not in Akpomville, it is the youngest person there that says the prayers. The rationale behind this was that the youngest is likely going to be the closest to God since he is likely going to be with fewer sins. It was then given to the priest. He, the priest, though a man of god declined to offer the prayers. He had insisted that the gods had heard enough from him and now it was time for another voice. It was therefore given to the oldest man there. By tradition in most of Utopia it was the oldest man present that did that job and so it was given to him. They thought that the indecision as to who would pray over the apple was over, but the old man was going to do his own.

He informed them that amber that is put into the palms of a child would never burn him. They knew exactly what he was saying. It was a proverb and what he was telling them is that he was about to delegate someone to do so. It was part of what made such prayers worth its while to watch. That was how it got back into the hands of the middle aged chief. Even then someone had shot up to protest. According to him, his clan was the oldest and there was no reason for the chief who came from the youngest clan to do so. He had insisted that for that reason honor should be bestowed to his clan, to which that honor was due. Technically it was a reasonable argument, but it was not a successful one. A few more heated, friendly and entertaining suggestions had been offered before the chief eventually did his job.

When the chief prayed, it had been to God and the other gods as well as all the ancestral spirits. It went like any other typical prayer but he also thanked them for what he saw—a lot of goods to point towards a bountiful harvest. He also prayed to their guardian spirits to keep to their jobs. He thanked all of them and a resounding AMEN followed.

The pieces of the apple that were eaten were to represent a symbol of peace and cooperation between them and the spirits. The auctioneering continued for just a few hours before dusk came and so the rest were stashed away to be sold the following day during the bazaar.

By dawn the following day, tarpaulin tents had miraculously sprung up all over the church premises. Various games and activities were to be held within them all day long and this was what the younger ones actually looked forwards to. Apart from the games, there were assorted foods, snacks and drinks everywhere and parents had given pocket money o their children for the day.

There were songs from various groups and there were dances. Every imaginable thing was on sale and at giveaway prices. It was essentially a Christian carnival.

By the end of the day almost everyone went home exhausted and happy while the younger carefree ones were all drunk. John Bottles, the village oaf and drunkard, had claimed that his most prominent feat for the day was the consumption of a local brew that had been mistakenly left unattended to after being stolen and stashed away. It had therefore fermented for over one year under the sun. Someone had forgotten it in the abandoned church graveyard where he found it. The emissaries were happy for once from what they had seen, though what went on inside the church amongst some of them was not too encouraging. They did not fail to notice that some of the younger ones were not there to worship, but to sort out members of the opposite sex.

The following day ushered in the two-day festival for the traditional thanksgiving. It was a festival to once more further thank the gods for a bountiful harvest. The first day was for the very young. It was the day that the children dressed up and went around visiting friends. Most parents stayed indoors and cooked to entertain these potential visitors. As these children went around, they were offered appetizing dishes which they could not refuse, and they were each full in no time. The rest of the day was therefore going to be spent expecting other gifts, and money was what they expected. Many had actually gone to the banks to withdraw money in small denominations for these children.

These children all carried small bags for their money and it was usually like a competition. They will each tally his or her takings at the end of the day and compare the totals. Whoever got the most amounts was regarded as the most liked in the village and probably the most influential too.

As for the men, they would be busy offering more of those harvests to the gods from their homes. Several choice animals will be slaughtered and the women will whip up all sorts of delicacies from these. Incidentally choice wines were always in abundance during this period.

This first day was therefore usually an uneventful day as such, except for the children and the younger adults who spent it visiting their friends for all sorts of reasons and gossips.

By the second day, it was time for the kids to be sentenced indoors and only peep through the windows. The older ones on the other hand were now out to burn off a few of the calories that they had acquired the previous three days. It was the day that the ancestral spirits manifested themselves and came out to entertain the people.

These ancestral spirits were never harmful and they were never wicked, but they will spend most of the day chasing the boys around with long whips. At times one boy or the other will try to impress the girls by offering to escort them past these spirits.

The day would actually start in the night when the spirit town crier, Ogbazuluobodo, would run round the village to announce the imminent appearance of his master, Ayaka. Ayaka was a mysterious spirit with immense magical powers, but he always remained invisible, except probably to members of its cult. It would simply go round the village in the dark without any single incidence unless someone was foolhardy enough to have light in his house. In that case it would give a warning that there was light in the house and if it is not turned off then he would act. In one such instance one stubborn man only woke up in the morning to find his car hanging precariously from a thin thread that was tied to the tip of a leaf far up the tree that was in his compound. In such instances he would have to meet with members of the cult and pay any fines they might impose and the car would miraculously come down once more.

At times it is hard to separate fantasy from truth, but he was claimed to have once transferred someone's house to the top of a great oak, or maybe Iroko, tree. The man only woke up in the morning to discover that he could not come out of his house. He was some two hundred feet away from the precious ground. He was also just an arms length from the low clouds, or heavens as he saw it. He had to call down on his neighbor to help him appease the spirit. It was only after the appeasement that he was let down.

Just before dawn the grand gossiper of the spirit world, whocalledme, came into the scene. He derived his name from the fact that he always wanted to gossip to humans but he could only appear at night when people were asleep. He would pretend that someone was calling him and start asking: 'who called me?' This would be an opportunity for him to drop some news of what was going on in the land of the humans. He would always shout: "who called me?" and then he would answer to the call and start a story.

It was through him that the village would find out those who were misbehaving, especially those who had committed adultery and fornication, for as a spirit he would know all these things. Not minding the fact that he would gossip on anything at all, he was essentially the indirect custodian of the village morals since whatever evil thing one did was going to be known by all.

It was for instance during one of those appearances that he told them what was going on with Paul. Paul was an old man who lived in the village and had lost most of his teeth, but could not afford a set of artificial dentures. He loved to eat meat and it was this spirit that informed the villagers that his wife suddenly turned into his grinder. She would chew the meat for him and then put it into his mouth for him to swallow. That was general fun, but then it was in the same breath that he informed them that the man's daughter was so obsessed with curly hair that she spent a lot of money for jerry curl on her armpit hairs, and yet her father had no teeth. The price for the curls was more than the price of a set of artificial teeth. He even pointed out that it was rumored that she did the same thing to her pubic hair.

There was another lady who was so promiscuous that it was this spirit who told the villagers how she used to cheat on her husband. He claimed that according to the grape vine, she used to make love to their security guard through a small round hole that she dug through the thin wall of their toilet that connected to the outside. When her husband discovered the hole, she insisted that a rat made it.

It was also from him that the villagers learnt of the exploits of Marina. She was the village beauty. Three different men were asking for her hand in marriage and he was the only person who could expose her. She was lying with each of them with the hope of choosing the best, and none suspected what was happening. Each of them thought that he was the only one for that was what she told each one.

Hardly had the suns golden rays begun to shoot across the horizon before the ubiquitous teenage spirits—Akatakas—began to run around. The village was situated atop a vast plateau and the sunrise had always been a beauty there. The early bronze had mildly hued the entire vista and it was only the harried footsteps of these manifested spirits that helped to wake the humans from their sweet dreams. This was going to be the last day of the four-day festival and it had always been the most exciting day.

These teenage spirits were everywhere and they were very agile with each one carrying a bunch of well-cured whips to add excitement to their chases. Except for those who had been initiated into the cult of the ancestral spirits, every other human was to be chased around. They were there to chase the people around but they were hardly ever flogged. The idea was to frighten people and the chase was just for the excitement. Once in a while their kid spirits would come around. These were ancestral spirits of the kids and they were each barely three feet six inches tall. They will therefore only prance around dancing to imaginary tunes and tones. These were the two sets of spirits that stayed on all day long. Young boys actually taunt them so that they could chase them around.

It was much later that the Ojionu would come out. He told funny stories and danced to very fast paced music. His music usually came from two or three accompanying humans with gongs, xylophones and flutes, with the flutes acting as the pace setters. His twin brother, the parrot, would often appear in a different area doing the same thing, but he was much more talkative.

Just after mid day the Okwonma appears. This was a spirit of a past heroic warrior. He was however regarded as the heroic coward of the spirit world. He always appeared with an oversized machete with which he frightened people, but he never uses it. It was actually rumored that he never used it and did not even know how to use it. Once in a while the spiritual impersonators of Agaba Idu and Ngbadike, two of the gods that we had seen earlier on will appear, each with the sole purpose of frightening people. Okwonma was their cousin.

This was a day of merriment and play, and people ran around all over the village, and by late afternoon most were already exhausted, men and spirits alike. The day would however not be over without the late arrival of three other ancestral spirits:

Agboghonmo and Agbonma, the twin sisters who were rumored to have been born by the same spirit that gave birth to Aphrodite were the first to appear. They were each as beautiful as, if not more beautiful, than Aphrodite. They just silently filed past the village for people to admire their beauty. It was from them that models learnt their catwalks. Their appearance usually signaled the next scenario. One would hear from the distance the entertaining music of the Akwunachienyi spirit.

The music came closer with each second that passed, and in no time at all the drummers would file past, all flamboyantly dressed. The spirit will then suddenly appear. It was a female spirit and she had an oversized head as well as an oversized tiara. When she appears, she would dance along to her music in intricate but measured steps. Humans lined all the roads to watch her dance past.

Her exit was only to heighten expectations—expectation of the appearance of the manifestable queen of the spirit world. Like her predecessor, her appearance is marked by the sound of her music. It was music not very much different from that of her predecessor, but it was more dignifying and more regal. As for her appearance, it is usually but for a very short period of time. She would appear in very slow, well measured and completely as well as mesmerizingly majestic steps that were fully synchronized to the music that came with him.

It is the musician with the gong that sets the pace for the dance steps together with the xylophonist. The drummers would respond, together with those beaded calabashes, cymbals and chimes, before the real star of the band, the flutist. He was usually the best flutist in the village and he could basically both sing and talk with his flute. He could produce tunes that will send excitement into any being, be he spirit or human, and those tunes could simply hypnotize the hearer.

On seeing him, one would understand why she usually appears but for a very short time only. She was very well dressed and her head was often as big as a small house. It was full of mirrors, various decorations, beads, rings, ornaments and other accoutrements that could each extract envy from the hearts of any lady.

The sun usually died down as she passed and that would mark the end of the fourth day of the festival. It would be a grand finale.

The gods were impressed by what they saw and what was going on in the village as regards the festivals and they went back home to report on that.

THE LEGAL FIELD

The next contingent to leave the heavens was headed by the learned Akawo, who happened to be the grand secretary general to the spiritual convocation. The duty of this group was to take a look into the human legal system.

This investigation was necessitated because they had not failed to notice the ways in which lawyers argued their cases in the court. Depending on whom he was representing, the same lawyer could view the same case from diametrically opposing sides. What he says is wrong in one case could be what he would profess to be right in the very next case. Some of the cases were cunningly entertaining while many were outrightly outrageous. They had decided to attend the hearings in a court at Utopia.

They were already within the courtroom when the judge made his carefree but impressively regal entry into the room. This particular judge was a portly and bald-headed man with protruding belly and eyes that seemed to be mere slits. His nose was large and the nostrils looked more like funnels, but whenever he spoke, it was with a slow and decisively assertive voice. He sat down before ordering every other person in the room to sit down too. They had all stood up earlier on to recognize his entry into the room. He then called on the court clerk to read out the cases for the day. There was only one case for that day, and the hooked nose lean clerk with a whispery but loud voice announced the case.

It was a complicated divorce case. It was complicated no matter how one looked at it. Professor John Doe was the man that was being sued by his wife, firstly for bigamy before divorce. He was being sued for divorce on the basis of unfaithfulness as well as bigamy. As if that was not enough the case of bigamy was based on the fact that he was, according to him, half gay, and also married to another man, the very reverend John Thomas. He was therefore a man with two wives, if the other man could be called a wife, and indeed their marriage certificate listed John Thomas as the wife. That was the terminology in the state where they contracted the marriage. To even make the issue less favorable for him, Rebecca was wedded to him in the Catholic Church while John was wedded to him at Saint Bottles Church.

To get the facts straight Rebecca sued him while eventually the other John also began to sue him as well.

The judge was known to be a very strict judge when it came to such cases, but John Doe had hired a very tough defense lawyer. His lawyer made it clear to the court that John was married to Rebecca and every one agreed with that. He now went on to explain to the court that the main issue was whether he was also married to the other John, and there the problem lay.

He then went on to point out to the court that the two Johns were married to each other but not as husband and wife. They were married to each other as partners, for no matter how one looked at it, though the government approved of such marriages; the legal definition of marriage is still between a man and a woman. If therefore he was not married to the other John, then the question of bigamy did not arise. If bigamy was therefore not an issue here, then there was no ground for divorce except for the issue of unfaithfulness, which he intended to address later.

Furthermore, he pointed out, Saint Bottle's church where they contracted the marriage as well was only one of the few churches that could do so. More pertinent to the issue was the fact that the church was not yet listed in the records of approved churches and so that marriage could as well be considered to be null and void.

When it came to the prosecutor, he did not buy the idea that when the two men got married it was not a marriage as such. According to him, John Thomas was a woman. He was just a woman that was trapped in a man's body and so he was technically a woman and so whatever was contracted between them was legal marriage. He finally asked everyone whether John Thomas should be punished for being a woman in a man's body and he gave the answer—no!

The defense rested its case by pointing out that that the union between John and Rebecca was a marriage between a man and a woman, but that in the case of the two Johns it was officially between two men and therefore simply a union and not a marriage. For this reason there was no way that he could be accused of having contracted two simultaneous marriages.

He however went on to point out too, that John was not unfaithful to Rebecca, because the law defined unfaithfulness in a specific manner. It was when a married person is found to be messing around with a person or persons that he was not married to. Since the prosecutor insisted that he was married to two people then he had no business accusing him of messing around outside of his marriage.

It was a brilliant argument and so the judge decided to give his ruling. He started off by pointing out that there had never been any judicial precedence to such a case and so he had been pushed to a tight corner. Going by the facts and technicalities of the case he was going to rule against his own conscience. He was going to rule in favor of the defense. John Doe was therefore not guilty of bigamy.

Now that the bigamy charge had been cleared, he wanted the pundits to address the remaining issue of divorce. It was two divorce cases against the same individual, one by his wife and the other by his partner.

When the defense lawyer stood up and cleared his throat to start, they were all ears, waiting to see what trick he was going to pull out of his legal hat this time around. He did not fail them.

He therefore started off by assuring the court that it had no jurisdiction over the case between the two Johns. He pointed out to the court that the marriage was contracted in a local government office and that the certificate was signed by the mayor who was eager to score a political point. Though the mayor was a lawyer by profession, he did not see how such a document could be deemed to be legally binding when the registry was there, together with the registrar who was paid to do that job. Furthermore, he pointed out that the document was worded in such a way as to indicate and confirm that the union was between a man and another man and not a marriage between them. Though the word marriage was mentioned in the document, it was not in such a manner as to indicate that what took place was an actual marriage. They were therefore domestic partners rather than spouses. Within that jurisdiction, the words marriage and union were interchangeable and each was loosely used.

To him, it was not therefore necessary to grant a divorce, what the court could do, would be to dissolve the agreement, or simply let them go their separate ways. He went on to point out that When John Thomas accused the other John of being unfaithful to him, he was wrong. He could be unfaithful to him only if he were with another man and the same applied to the case that Rebecca had brought forward. He finally came up with a simple analogy to drive home his point:

According to him, drinking water and eating a bowl of low carbohydrate rice both together constitute eating. Each could easily lead to satiety and yet they are not exactly the same. If one were therefore still dieting and decides to eat a bowl of rice cooked in sugar solution, in place of the low carbohydrate rice he would surely have cheated. The cheating would however be on the rice but not on the water. It is the same as the situation between John, Rebecca and John. John Doe had not cheated on anyone.

The judge did not buy that argument and it did not lead to anywhere as far as he was concerned. To him whatever it tied can always be untied no matter who tied it in the first instance or even when and where it was tied. He was going to dissolve both unions. The judge hinted that he was going to grant divorce to each of them not minding that the church might frown at that. He was going to kill two birds with one stone, as he put it.

Before the judge could finish the case each of the aggrieved had decided to pay John Doe back in his own coins. It was during the case that John Thomas found out that he was not fully gay. He fell in love with Rebecca right there and the judge did not waste time to tie the knot for them.

The emissaries were not surprised at what had taken place in the courtroom. They had long known that man was capable of utilizing his powers of straight and crooked thinking to manipulate situations around him. The lawyers, and of course politicians were the best at that. They then decided to enter the circuit court to find out what was happening there, but it did not fare better. The situation there was even worse.

There, it was a case where a man had stolen his neighbor's car. He did so having surrendered his neighbor with his hunting knife. It was therefore a clear case of armed robbery.

As was usual with these criminals, the man was able to hire a smart criminal attorney. On investigation, it was found out that he had cut his neighbor with the knife in four different places. The lawyer had insisted that it was not his client that cut his neighbor. According to him it was the knife and so he did not see why they should leave the actual culprit and face this poor innocent man.

The prosecutor, as well as the judge, pointed it out to him that the knife was an inanimate object and so it was the person holding it that should be found guilty. He agreed with the judge that it was his client that held the knife but the problem is that he was not the person that controlled its movement. Just as his client took possession of the knife, so did the devil take possession of his client and so the devil should be found guilty instead.

The judge then decided to trap him with his own argument, but he was too smart for the court. The judge then asked him to produce the culprit so that they could release his client. He hardly thought it over before agreeing to that. He however informed the judge that since the state had the responsibility of bringing in accused people, he would aid them in that after they had paid the bill for such and it was going to be very expensive. When the judge told him that he was only technically correct because he had to bring him in before they paid him, he brought out his master plan.

Now that the judge had agreed that the devil was the culprit he came up with a totally different solution: The devil was a spirit that existed in the other world and they had no extradition treaty with them. Moreover he also dwelt outside their area of jurisdiction. Even then, they had no jurisdiction over him.

The judge had been trapped and so he could not help it but to agree to throw away that portion of the charges. The man did not injure his neighbor.

As for the charge of stealing the car, the defender insisted that his client had all intentions of returning it and he had proofs for that. He was only there to borrow the car. When asked for the proof that he had, he produced a handwritten note from the accused, which he had intended to give to the victim. In it he had written that he just wanted to borrow the car for an emergency and that it was going to be for just about fifteen minutes. According to him the reason why the victim did not receive the note is that he was harassed his client into defending himself, and so the incidence did not end as he had planned.

He was only found partially guilty and the judge sentenced him to time served while awaiting trial.

To the emissaries, this was a gross miscarriage of justice and it went to prove that in the attempt to make money, these lawyers were capable of twisting facts at will. Lying had become institutionalized and they were not very happy with that situation.

THE SHRINE OF SAINT BOTTLES CHURCH

We were created for the pleasure of the gods and so they have always been interested in knowing how we plan to get close enough to them. This meant that they had to be interested in how they were being worshiped. There seem to be many religions and many ways of reaching out to our creator but the important thing seemed to be how close each person comes to Him.

This set of emissaries was therefore sent out to the churches. If you have seen one then you have seen them all. This does not mean that they did the same thing, but whatever took place pointed to what men had in mind. It was once more to that Saint Bottles Church of Bacchus that they went. The peculiar thing about this church was that the priest officiated from a high podium smack in the middle of the church rather than from one end as was usual.

Since this church was dedicated to the god Bacchus, it was obvious that their main activity had to be connected with wine. Most normal churches had their seating arranged as regular pews from the back to the front, but this was not a normal church. It's seats were made up of numerous tables with chairs arranged around each. It was on these tables that the congregants communed.

On this particular day the priest said the opening prayers before they fell to the order of the day. Most of the churches fully communed with their makers once a week and for just a few hours each time. Here it was all week long and the services lasted all day long. He started off by breaking bread, in this case it was just to pray over a few kola nuts, which they broke into pieces and ate with the spirits. He prayed for the gods to always forgive them their sins, especially those that were committed knowingly, since to them, any sins that were committed unknowingly were not strictly speaking sins. He pointed out that the adulteration of the drinks was definitely a sin that had been premeditated. This was a serious sin, according to him, since when their master turned water into wine he did set an example for them. He made sure that it was the best wine that was produced. It was an example for all to emulate and they should follow in his footsteps.

He then thanked them for being kind enough to keep them alive and at least well enough for them to return to pay further homage to them. He then continued the prayers not just with thanks but also with pleas for their jobs and more bountiful harvests for the farmers. This was necessary so that more drinks could be available and also so that they would have enough money to buy them. He finally called on them to be in their mists so as to guide and guard them through their deliberations. They then fell on the drinks.

At Saint bottles church, charity was not an issue. Passers by were at times invited in to sample one or two cups free. It was this gesture that expressed how charitable they could be. They did not have any church collections.

At the nearby Saint Johnson's Church, it was a different story. They had an elaborate charitable organization. This was a church that also believed that charity began at home. One could always deduce what that meant. They had a couple of church collections and one of them was for their charitable organization. The mode of disbursement of the money so collected had always remained a questionable affair. The priest was the one who had the onus to prove to them that charity began at home and for that reason most of the funds so raised were allocated to his girl friends and concubines.

They also had a charitable organization, which took care of refugees. This particular charity raised extra money through companies that wanted to cheat the government when it came to paying taxes. The charitable donations to them were deductible from their taxes. These people used to bring the money to this organization through the church and that was for a very good reason. They were to kill two birds with the same stone—giving to the gods and cheating the government. It was from this money that he started off to purchase and maintain a fleet of executive jets that would enable him visit all over the world where the refugees might be. He had never been to any of the refugee camps but he claimed that he always prayed for them while flying over them.

He finally managed to open the 'charitable bank of necromancy.' This bank gave out loans without collaterals, and it also did not charge any interests on its loans. He secured more money for the loans from government grants for this unique bank. What was the catch? The bank was built at the gate of a massive cemetery. He was giving the loans to the souls of the dearly departed and so most of them ended up as delinquent loans. Since these souls had no need for physical money, he always helped them out to spend their money.

This issue of charity was enough to make the gods know that whenever it came to the issue of charity, man was not to be trusted. The churches were in effect business enterprises, though with a few exceptions.

Back to saint bottles church. After the prayers, the priest had taken a very generous sip from his cup, swirled it round in his mouth before swallowing it with a loud smack to indicate that it was a very good vintage. This was what took place before the congregants began to imbibe. There was every conceivable drink there, as long as it was alcoholic. It seemed that the object of the drinking was for each person to drink enough to make him get closer to the spirits either through dreams or visions or even speaking in tongues. It did not really matter which spirit they were after, but the spirit that dwelt in bottles always came to them first.

Most of them in the spirit will stagger and often fall down and a few will have convulsions. This was the manifestation of the possession by the spirits and it could be a good spirit or maybe an evil one since any spirit is capable of possessing people.

When an evil spirit possesses one, it is simply referred to as possession, but if it happens to be a good spirit then he is simply in the spirit. If he speaks in an unknown tongue when possessed by an evil spirit then he is babbling incoherently, but for the good spirit, it is speaking in tongues. Now, talking of speaking in tongues it really makes no difference whether it is tongues or babbling.

For the Christians it is actually a good thing to be able to speak in tongues for it is a gift from God as noted here:

"Now there are diversities of gifts, but the same spirit."

(1 Corinthians Ch 12, Vs 4)

"… to another divers kinds of tongues; to another the interpretation of tongues."

(1 Corinthians Ch 12, Vs 10}

However without the gift to interpret, the other would be useless as the same bible went on to further clarify:

> "So likewise ye, unless you utter by the tongue words easy to be understood, how shall it be known what is spoken? For ye shall speak into the air."
>
> (1 Corinthians Ch 14, Vs 9)

For this reason those speaking in tongues are not necessarily doing any good or contributing to the spiritual upliftment of the rest. This is obvious if one went further down that very same passage:

> "Yet in the church I had rather speak five words with my understanding, that by my voice I might tech others also, than ten thousand words in an unknown tongue."
>
> (1 Corinthians Ch 14, Vs 19)

I am saying all these because it follows that in all the churches, people are speaking in tongues and how can one tell that it is not an evil spirit if he cannot understand what is being said. Supposing you understand that the spirit just asked you to go to hell then you would right away start to suspect that it is an evil spirit. It is for this reason that it went on to further explain:

> "If any man speak in an unknown tongue, let it be by two, or at most three, and that by course; and let one interpret."
>
> (1 Corinthians Ch 14, Vs 28}

It is not that there is something wrong with speaking in tongues, but since there is generally no interpreter, it might be better for one to do it in private as a communion between him and his maker, This is supported by the verse that went:

> "But if there be no interpreter, let him keep silence in the church; and let him speak to himself, and to God."
>
> (1 Corinthians Ch 14, Vs 28}

It is therefore obvious that speaking in tongues was common in both Saint Bottles church and the other Christian churches. The difference is that it seems to be more in the previous case. This is however totally different from the one that was spoken by the apostles on the day of Pentecost. In their own case speaking in tongues was a totally different thing. In their own case they spoke and everyone heard then in their own tongues as explained in the two following passages from the same bible:

> "And they were all filled with the Holy Ghost, and began to speak with other tongues, as the spirit gave them utterance."
>
> (Acts Ch 2, Vs 4)

> "And how hear we every man in our own tongue, wherein we were born?"
>
> (Acts Ch 2, Vs 8)

It is obvious that in the case of the apostles on the day of Pentecost, speaking in tongues was probably on a totally different platform. They simply spoke in their own dialect and everyone present heard and understood in his or her own native language.

Whichever way one went, the issue seemed to be a battle between good and evil, and it all depends on what one saw as good or as evil, depending once more on his own peculiar interpretation and culture. That was why religion was there to show which is which. It is obvious that one could be possessed by either of these spirits and if one therefore happened to be made by either of them to speak in tongues then it would be a case of pure exercise in futility if there were none to interpret the utterances.

The only reason that I am going to such extent about speaking in tongues is because of those who spoke in them. It is because of pastors who exploit that phenomenon to the fullest, usually for fame, deception and other personal gains. Without being possessed, these priests spoke in tongues, which are unknown not even to themselves and definitely not even by the gods. They simply make up those well-rehearsed words and shout them during prayers and healing sessions. The emissaries were opportune to watch one preacher do just that, and all they could do was to promise him that his reward would come later.

It had been an all day event at the Saint Bottles Church, and each adherent was free to go home as soon as he feels that he had attained enlightenment. This is often evidenced by lightheadedness and dizziness. This, according to their rules, meant that the spirit was already beginning to come into them. By late afternoon, most of them had left, though new congregants replaced them, and a new high priest had taken over for the second shift. Some had stayed longer than others while some were more drunk than others. It was not really drunkenness since they considered it possession by the spirits not minding the fact that it could have been by that set of spirits that dwelt within the bottles. To them a spirit is a spirit.

It was a very lively congregation all day long and each person was free to contribute to the grapevine. Stories abounded, some true and others false, and even amongst the true ones, many had received their fair shares of embellishments. In other words it was a gossip forum.

It was during one of these mini sessions that they learnt that a politician had just deposited a large amount of money in some foreign accounts. Some were in his name, some in his wife's name, some in his girlfriend's name and most amazingly, one was in the name of a child that he hoped to have in about three years time. It was not that the spirits did not know about the man, but it was the human version of the incident that was new to them.

The politician was the secretary to the department of housing and construction. Ninety billion dollars was released for a massive construction project and as soon as the money got into the account that he controlled he made his move. Jobs were created and surveys made. Award letters were issued as well as completion certificates and within a month, all the money had been paid out. Everything was just on paper and nothing really happened. All the foreign accounts had the same signatory and that was himself.

When he was accosted for the issue, he simply abandoned his job and fled the country. To show how smart he was, he fled from Utopia to Newt. The two villages were sworn enemies and so there was no way that they were going to catch up with him.

Though the congregants told this story as if the worst had taken place, it was really nothing. It had come to be their acceptable way of life. Were any of them to be elected into office, he would do the same thing—grab as much as you could and find your way out. To them, it was public money and public money enjoyed the same fate as holy water in the font at the back entrance of any church. It was free and fair game for any passerby who could stick his finger into it. It would be a missed opportunity not to do so. Cheating and the mismanagement of public funds, as well as corruption had become endemic and now ingrained in them and they had realized that only a radical measure could redeem them.

Now back to Saint Johnson's Church. Though Aphrodite went into Saint Bottles, they did not notice her. At Saint Johnson's, it was a different story. Most of the congregation had their eyes as well as ears on her. They did not hear a single word that the priest uttered. It was not their fault for who were they not to be distracted when the priest himself was distracted as well. He was so into her that he did not realize that he had ended a prayer with: "in the name of this beauty, and her body and her hypnotic face; amen." He was already planning on how to get her. The strategy that had worked for him before would be to invite her to the confessional and then let her confess to any sin. He would then get her to come to his house for some penance.

He had always been like that. It was not until many of the girls and some married women began to give birth to babies of mixed blood that the bishop arranged for his transfer. It was a Caucasian congregation and he was black. Incidentally it is not all the priests that were like that. In his own case he always preached on, and against divorce. The reason is that it was the bitterness of his own divorce that drove him to the priesthood. As would be expected, it was his wife that sued for the divorce on the grounds that he was addicted to unfaithfulness.

The reverend mother that often assisted him did not fare any better. She had been divorced three times before the calling. In each case, her chastity had been called into question, while her faithfulness to her marital vows and obligations almost always faltered. The picture would not be complete if it is not pointed out that she had five children, all while married. Unfortunately, they were from five different men and she was never married to any of those five. She had all of them out of wedlock while being married, if one could put it that way.

After this they came to the final conclusion that most men of god, as they were known, were just there to exploit the people just for a few dollars more. That did not however make them take pity on the masses that were being deceived. Each man had claimed that power to know the difference between good and evil and so to be misguided by these charlatans was not an excuse. They had been advised that by their fruits they shall know them.

TRANSPORTATION

One might wonder why the gods should be interested in transportation when they could conveniently materialize wherever and whenever they wished. The fact is that only the human spirit could do that but not the body. They were therefore interested in finding out how man coped with this particular inadequacy. He had been imbued with the power of ingenuity and it was his lot to invent what he had to use.

Mercury was chosen to represent them in this investigation. It was not just because he was already used to it, but it actually fell within his own department, after all he was the messenger of the gods.

It was claimed that for reasons of first hand experience they started off the journey aboard an Unidentified Flying Object. It was a vehicle that they had chartered from Galaxy X. This was a galaxy that was occupied by beings that were more advanced than humans, but then they were not equal to the gods. They were not created exactly in the image of the gods, as one of them had rightly or wrongly claimed, but their vehicles were different from our own. Their crafts operated by electromagnetic principles and the energy stone, which was found only in that galaxy, generated the power that they needed.

As soon as they got close to the earth, they were dropped off at the international space station from where they proceeded down to earth in a spacecraft. The craft had put them down somewhere in Acadia, and it was from there that they took a Jumbo jet to Utopia. The first class section of the plane was as good as empty but they rode in the economy class. This was to enable them experience what the masses felt. In fact there were only two men in the entire twenty seat first class section. They were company chief executive officers on an errand. It beat the gods to note this fact. Why did they provide those seats that were bound to be empty when the economy class was overbooked? Why not reduce its size and get more passengers? No wonder they always tend to go bankrupt. Many of them actually raise fares in order to survive.

The jet was one and a half hours late before taking off. The delay was initially blamed on a computer crash before it came to a broken conveyor belt later on. It however eventually took off. It was an uphill task to keep the passengers on their seats during take off. They roamed about at will, and some could be seen standing about in groups for discussions that usually bordered on politics. It was going to be a ten-hour flight and so some were actually moving around just to loosen up. The cabin crew on their part did not do much about this. It was because they did not want it to seem that they were not polite to their customers, after all, the customer is always right. One of them actually went jogging along the aisles.

When it was time for the meals, a few of them made fairly outrageous demands. One lady asked for both tea and coffee at once while her friend asked for wine, beer and champagne all at once. One claimed that he was a heavy eater and so he demanded for three plates of food. All these were however done in an attempt to extract the most out of the exorbitant fare that they had paid.

It was not until the fasten seat belt lights came on as they went through some air turbulence that a few of them decided that it was time to use the restrooms. Whenever they were asked to sit down, they will grumble loudly in protest about how they were being pressed and in fact one lady threatened to ease herself right there in the middle of the aisle.

Many were extremely careless during the meals. Thrash was littered all around on the floor and the entire cabin was an eyesore. As for the spirit visitors, they remained invisible all through the flight.

Not long after they arrived at the Utopian international airport, they took public transportation to make it to the seaport, which was some two hundred miles away. It was an airport taxi that took them to the place.

They had hardly cleared the city before the smartly dressed chauffeur took of like a jet plane. To be fair to him, he did not beat any red traffic lights while in the city. The speed limit on the freeway was sixty-five miles per hour, but he was already doing eighty. He was however not the only culprit when it came to speed. Many of the trailers and tankers were flying past at eighty-five miles per hour. Most of these big vehicles were going at this speed despite the fact that most of them were actually overloaded. This was the main reason why they used to have a lot of inexplicable accidents along this road.

It was not quite fifteen minutes before the traffic came to a standstill. A big tractor-trailer had jack-knifed and blocked the road. It had fallen on its side. To make matters worse, it was carrying a load of hazardous materials. The backup was already about five miles long. The taxi man was irritated and openly agitated as he swore his voice hoarse. It eventually took the better part of three hours for the fire trucks and other emergency responders to clear the mess and pull the monster vehicle off to the side of the road.

At times these accidents are caused by the quality of the drivers themselves as well as the nature of the roads. It was later that they learnt that the trailer driver was just barely a month into the job, having failed his driver's license test more than a couple of times. The first time that he failed the test, he had run through a red light. His explanation to the testing officer was that he thought that red meant that he should drive on. In another instance he was so drunk before the test that as soon as he got into the vehicle he did not waste time before asking the testing officer what that round thing in front of him was. It was the steering wheel.

This was not the only probable cause of these accidents. Excessive speed was on cause. Every driver was in a hurry to get to his destination, if possible even before taking off. Another problem was the nature of the cars on the roads. The local economy had so deteriorated that they were beginning to import used cars. At first there were restrictions as to the age and conditions of the cars that were allowed into the village. One politician however took pity on the poor masses just before an election. He wanted everyone to be able to afford a car, and so he made it a new rule that the condition and age of the cars no longer mattered. What followed was a complete calamity.

People began to bring in anything that they came across. Many actually went to junkyards to resurrect a couple of cars and import them into Utopia. These were junks that were about to be recycled for scrap metal. These were essentially death traps. Some lost their tires at high speed and every conceivable scenario was possible. In fact one had lost its engine at high speed the other day. The engine simply fell off.

Despite the fact that the accident rate had quadrupled due to this political maneuver, the poor supported the politician and voted him in for another term in office. One of such cars had actually overtaken them on the road and they did not fail to notice that its gas tank cover was just a wad of green leaves. The chauffeur had told them of one of such cars that was right in front of him the other night. It had no trafficator lights and so the driver was using a flashlight. He stuck it out and was switching it off and on to indicate that he was about to turn left.

Apart from these faults they were still preferred since they were imported cars. The reason for this was that the Utopian manufactured vehicles often had problems of their own. The first car that they manufactured always burst into flames even with minor collisions. Apart from this the owners of these cars spent more time with the mechanics than they did driving them. To add to these problems, they were all gas-guzzlers. Rather than try to improve on their record, they got the government, through lobbying—mind you this is not bribery, to rule that all government official cars had to be that very model.

People protested at such corruption and so they went on to improve on their records. The next model that came out was the one whose tires always burst at high speed. Many people had lost their lives before an investigation into that began. It was found out that their tires were not properly manufactured and so they faced the tire manufacturing company. It was soon discovered that it was the car manufacturer who, in an effort to cut costs, had asked the tire manufacturer to omit four out of the five layers that they used to apply in the manufacturing process. The car company was indigenous and the tire company foreign and so it was the tire maker that was found guilty of manufacturing substandard tires and they were fined for that. The car manufacturer was only trying to save costs.

That was not all. The next model had problems with its braking system. A case in question was when a drive decided to go home from the church after a service. He had started the engine, put the gear lever in drive to move further away from the car parked next to him before he could reverse properly. When he pressed down on the accelerator, the car went forwards as expected and then he tried to brake, but it kept going. He therefore pressed down further on the brake pedal but instead of stopping, the car sailed forwards through the wall and into the church. It was the altar table that eventually stopped it.

It was not until the priest had dashed out to thank god that someone had just donated a new car to the church that the driver discovered that the steering wheel had also detached and was in his hands. The first fault was that the brake and accelerator pedals were connected to the same lever system with a computer chip there to decide on which was needed at a particular time. It was just a computer glitch that caused the problem. As for the steering wheel, they had forgotten to put in any nuts to hold it down!

It was obvious from all that had happened so far that man was not interested in his own safety or life. He was more interested in money, and money by all means.

Despite all these, the chauffeur managed to extricate himself from the traffic jam and with a ninety-five mile an hour speed they were soon at the harbor, though much later than they had planned. They had noticed that the road was rather busy. This was because it was the peak passenger season, which was the period that most people were headed for islands towards the equator for some heat. This was also part of the reason why there were so many accidents. Many of the vehicles were also overloaded, as they squeezed one more passenger into any possible space. Some were actually standing in the larger vehicles such as busses due to lack of any more seats.

At the seaport they boarded a ferry to the island portion of Utopia. The ferry was a moving disaster. It ran aground when the captain was busy attending to his mobile phone and missed the route. It was at that moment that the engine also stalled. A tugboat eventually pulled them out, but just at that moment, his steering and navigation system developed its own problem. The compass would not work either and so the helmsman decided to follow the stars now that it was getting dark. Unfortunately for them, he was not a particularly bright or intelligent fellow. He had chosen the wrong star and so they went west instead of east.

Eventually he ended up in a sand bar and so a hot air balloon was sent from a nearby horseracing course to fly them to shore. It was one calamity after the other and one stupidity after the next. The basket was not properly tied to the balloon and so it eventually took off into the air without them.

Our emissaries had experienced more than they bargained for and so they decided to materialize at their destination and then did the same thing to get home. They were convinced that when it came to transportation, the humans were as inefficient as one could be.

SCHOOLING

"Knowledge is power" had been the most popular slogan in Utopia, and they were right for illiteracy was like a mooring that could hold one back. The next set of emissaries was therefore sent down to take a look at a school in Utopia. Acada, the patron saint of those who were interested in learning and the god of education was the head of the delegation. His assistant was his very opposite. He was itibolibo, the dunce—one is yet to figure out how he got that name. He was the patron saint of those who were academically challenged.

As a godling, Itibolibo was a never-do-well, and he was such a failure when it came to the acquisition of knowledge that he actually spent an entire ten years in year three of the celestial elementary school. He was not just the oldest in the class but he was old enough to be the father of most of the others who fared better than him in the class. It did not really boarder him because he always boasted that he was the most experienced pupil in the class. He even claimed that the senior gods were very unfair to him because they should have already started paying him as a professional student.

The school got so fed up with him that they just had to award him a pass to get him out of that class, and it was claimed that it was because of him that the celestial government introduced the 'no child left behind' policy. They had introduced the automatic promotion system into their school system. First of all it made more pupils to pass out, but more importantly it ensured that they did not have to throw in more money into the school system. For some to fail meant that they would repeat and so more students will be in the school. This of course meant more money, which they did not plan to spend. It might be more attractive to embezzle it.

A couple of muses were also included in the group and they decided to visit the Comprehensive Desideratum High School in Akpomville. They had chosen this particular school because it had classes that ranged from nursery school through university level.

A class was chosen at random and when they entered, it tuned out to be a practical chemistry class. The students were at the final stages of their project on the production of alcohol. This was a very important lesson because the government was beginning to toy with the idea of mixing their petrol with alcohol in order to reduce their overdependence on the importation of petroleum products. It was going to be like the killing of two birds with one stone since that would also lower the emission of gasses that were harmful to the earth's ozone layer. This had been blamed for the dramatic change in the world climate.

They had been given five cups each of corn, soybeans and rice. Their project was to produce alcohol from each of these and then decide on which one would yield the highest amount. One of the students had reported that his experiment did not produce any alcohol at all. The most successful of the students was the one that brought in about two teaspoonfuls of alcohol from each.

The explanation for those results was obvious, and that had made their professor mad! He had been deprived of the opportunity of sampling each product orally as the most reliable method of assay to determine the quality of alcohol being produced. That portion of the experiment was for him. For this failure of the students to perform, he ended up being the only sober person in the class. The entire class was drunk. That went to show how seriously they took scientific investigations.

It was even a bigger shock when they went into the next class. It was a sex education class. The government had made sex education compulsory for all ten year olds in schools. This had become their most favorite subject and it was because of this that many of them went to school at all. Their teacher was a pretty twenty-one year old blonde who was there for her teaching internship. She had finished with the syllabus before one of the students went ahead to convince her that sex education being a part of biology, it will never be complete without experimentation. Biology was a science and experiments were the basis of scientific pursuits.

She was a free spirited young girl and quite adventurous. She had always had her eye on one eleven-year-old boy in the class and so she decided that it was time for her to demonstrate for them. They eagerly did so on the class table while the rest were free to follow suit, and learn from her methods. In no time at all, it turned into a sex orgy class. The teacher was eventually charged with the rape of a minor.

It was while the orgy was going on behind closed doors that the emissaries walked through the wall into the classroom. They were both shocked and outraged. It was a blatant disregard to one of the commandments—thou shall not commit adultery. For her, it was not adultery. It was just a scientific experiment. They did not blame her altogether since it was the government that started it, for how could one explain their obsession with sex education.

When they moved into the physics class, the class was already over, but the teacher was demonstrating an experiment for one of his students. He was trying to explain to her the theory that light travelled in a straight line and that normal light would not penetrate most opaque solid objects no matter how thin. The room was dim, and on the table he had mounted a lighting device that was able to produce just a narrow beam of light. For the purposes of the experiment, she had to bare her chest and the beam was directed to her left nipple as a second phase. He took photographs of the whole thing both with her blouse on and without it. First of all they could see the beam of light travelling in a straight line in the dark. The second part was to inspect the photographs. The light could not penetrate her blouse in the first instance, which was his control, but it showed the nipple in the second experiment. The gods knew exactly what was going on and so they quickly proceeded to the next class.

This time around it was an economics class and they were discussing finance. The teacher had posed a question to his students: "Assuming that your mother was to go to a market that was about ten miles away, which would be the best way to get there considering the cost of transportation?

    (a) By land where the bus—fare would be fifteen dollars to the bus stop and another three dollars for taxi from the bus stop to the market, which was not exactly along the bus route.

    (b) By sea since the market was down the river and the fare for the ferry would be sixteen dollars.

    (c) By air which will cost ten dollars and another five dollars from the airstrip to the market by taxicab.

    (d) By foot, which would cost nothing at all, though she will get to the market after it had closed.

    (e) None of the above—explain.

Almost all the students chose the last option as the correct answer. Their explanation was also almost the same. They were of the opinion that each of the first four answers was correct since the monetary involvement was low. The catch however was that the cost would be negative if one were to sell his mother in the market.

It was therefore obvious that for man money was foremost in his list of priorities. They were ready to sell their mothers for money. It did not seem to be their fault because the village actually translated any given situation in terms of monetary gains. It therefore followed that the country itself, as well as its inhabitants, were evil since according to that holy book:

"For the love of money is the root of all evil . . ."

(1 Timothy Ch 6, Vs 10)

The spirits felt that they had seen enough, but they still had to visit those in the university environment. These students were taking their final examinations. Everyone in the room was a cheat. Some had copied out important information in their palms. The wiser ones left their palms alone since the questions were, oftener than not, so complicated that they sweated in their palms. These were the ones that went for their arms, legs and even breasts as well as all sorts of pieces of paper. When the one that had copied mathematical formulae on her left breast was caught she quickly covered it and exposed the other breast. On that one she had written: "I love you." She was a fairly pretty girl and the invigilator simply swallowed hard and let her go.

The more technologically savvy set texted the questions to another professor who texted the correct answers back to them for a fee. Others contributed money to give to the deviant professor and then they took photographs of the questions and sent them to him as an e-mail. He mailed the answers back to them.

It was among this set that one lecturer had problems with once. One of the students had asked his mother to help him out and so she visited the professor at home during the exam to pay him in kind. He was so involved with her that he mailed back wrong answers to them. They all failed. In retaliation however, they kidnapped him and forced him to give them a check, which they cashed before releasing him. It was for all his life savings. He had earlier on tried to defend himself by claiming that he had been paid by them to help them answer the questions, which he did. They did not specify as to whether the answers had to be correct or wrong.

In another instance, one lecturer was trying his hands at hacking when he chanced upon his students mailing questions to another lecturer. He intercepted the e-mails and sent back wrong answers to them. To make sure that the person for whom the mails were intended for was not going to be blamed, he told them what he had done. Of course they all failed.

It was not only the students that cheated. The teachers did their own bit too. When the government decided to start promoting the teachers based on the performance of their students they took immediate action. Many of them multiplied the results by a factor that they called the achievement factor. With that some of the students scored well over a hundred percent but that was allowable in their system of education, When it came to external examinations, they helped their students out during the examinations.

This did not just stop with the teachers. Federal government education monetary allocations to states were based on state scores in examinations. Utopia was not going to be deprived of this money and so they simply lowered the pass mark in their examinations and everyone passed.

It was therefore obvious that man would cheat when it came to the field of education, and he would do so without looking back. Their report pointed out that the preoccupation with money had made education irrelevant. It is claimed that the road to hell was wide and straight while that to heaven was narrow and winding. Man had chosen the former. He wanted every thing as easy as possible and would not mind enjoying now and going to hell later. He had opted for the easier alternatives, money and immorality. The acquisition of knowledge used to be the main preoccupation of schools but now it had not only been relegated to the background; it had been abandoned altogether.

GOVERNANCE

So far it had been unsatisfactory and so it was time to see how man governed himself. Mercury had previously given a detailed report of this in The Echoes of Yesteryears, and so this time around, the idea was to see whether there had been any changes for the better.

God had made man in his own image, we were told, and so he eventually developed that freedom of choice. Though they had laid down rules for men to follow, they did not seem to follow them. It was the Greeks that started it all when they came up with the idea of democracy and then the Romans sort of perfected it. Now it was the turn of Acadia. They infused freedom and rights into it and that came to be the birth of modern democracy with all its attendant ills.

Man, as had been pointed out, had acquired that power to reason and decide, and so after Lucifer was banished from the heavens and driven down to keep him companion, he grew wings. It was he who materialized as a snake to tempt Eve in the Garden of Eden. That signaled the beginning of the downfall of man. That was why man was able to reason with the devil do introduce democracy into all aspects of his life. It should be remembered that god actually gave the rules before the advent of this democracy.

It is a certain idea that without those Greek philosophers democracy would never have been. This was the group that could prove or disprove anything, even the same thing. They could for instance prove that black was white and then go on to disprove it. They were the forerunners of the lawyers who were normally capable of proving that wrong is right and that right is wrong, as well as that wrong is wrong and that right is right. This was the group that controlled the field of politics in Acadia. Utopia learnt this from them.

It was therefore not surprising when the Utopians made sure that their government was built on a foundation of religion while at the same time making sure that religion was kept apart from that very same government. It was for this reason that they could make a pledge of allegiance to their flag with emphasis on the fact that they were one nation under God and then go right ahead to explain that religion—or even the idea of God—was to be left alone. In effect this was the group that could conveniently talk from either side of their mouths, and it is they that have shaped politics and governance.

That was how they came up with that idea that marriage was the union between a man and a woman while at the same time making sure that a man could marry another man or a woman another woman without the noun marriage used for them. This time around it would be a union. The emissaries did not fail to notice this—they were both unions.

That was how they always managed to swear in their officials as well as themselves in the name of God while whatever they do should be kept away from the same very God. Incidentally God and religion happen to be the sole custodian of morality and so it follows that by keeping him away, they were simply ordaining immorality. In fact theocratic governments, which are those that put god in control were immediately attacked and democracies introduced to them. Some had regarded this trend as an attempt by Acadia to lead everyone to hell, and they were not wrong.

Apart from corruption, which was only normal here, there were two vices that were their major preoccupations: sex and money. For better comprehension, whatever anyone or even the government did was usually reduced to monetary terms. In effect government policies had to reflect this. Take for instance the idea of what drug the government should pay for. A lot of its citizens were suffering from deadly cancer, but take a look at what group of drugs they chose to make free. With cancer, the patient may die and save them money, but when it came to pregnancy, there will be more births and so they will spend more money. It was for this reason that they chose to make contraceptives alone free. They insisted that the idea was not to promote sex, but the people hailed them for letting them have sex without the fear of pregnancy. To the gods however, they were only promoting immorality.

Because Acadia and now Utopia were a freewill zone where anything was possible, that s anything bad, there was that tendency for people to flock into them. They therefore presently had an unprecedented influx of foreigners.

As they were about to leave, they found out that there was a function going on in a school coliseum and so they decided to find out what was going on there. It was a group of politicians who opposed the present government that were campaigning towards an oncoming election.

There were about twelve contestants and each had erected a tent outside the coliseum where they provided food and refreshment for their respective supporters. Some gave out free shirts with their names and photographs on them to whoever they came across. They mingled with their fans before going into the hall to make powerful speeches that were usually full of promises and verbose words but without substance or sincerity. Though they were there to vote and give the party an idea, or at least the semblance of an idea, of who was the most popular amongst the candidates, they were charged fifty dollars each to vote. It was a way of raising money for the party from its supporters. That is what democracy was all about.

The candidates were each allowed only a short time to speak and so they were forced to go straight to their points. Their aim was simply to find out how to unseat the ruling party no matter how good they have been to the village. They took actions that were meant to make the ruling party bad even if they were making the village to collapse. The important thing was that they should win. This is probably because the ruler is usually in a better position to make money, after all politics was their profession and that was the only way that they could make money. Even if the people they were planning to rule would suffer from their actions, it did not matter for it is the end that justifies the means. They always used the word patriotic, but what they meant was that they were patriotic to themselves and to their individual pockets.

Democracy was the government of the people, by the people and for the people, and this was how one of the politicians explained it: this is a government of the people for we are all Utopians, by the people for we have been elected by the people one way or the other, and for the people since our individual pockets are being taken care of and we are part of the people.

The government was in fact so insensitive to the needs and aspirations of its people that when the people complained of an unemployment rate that was too high they immediately took action. One of their socially oriented departments, which employed well over a million people, was immediately modernized. They spent money to import a few robots to do most of the work, and in no time at all they lost over half of their work force to those robots. They claimed that they did not want other villages to look more modernized than they were. The unemployment rate of course went up much higher than before. The catch is that a few made a lot of money from the contracts while many got theirs from the lobbing process.

It was also at this very moment that they decided to cut taxes for the big manufacturers, the rationale behind it being that it was going to be an incentive for them to hire more workers so that production would rise. Protagonists of this idea wanted to know who was going to buy the extra products since there was no money in circulation, but it fell on deaf ears. Of course no company hired an extra hand because they knew that pumping more money into the production of unsellable goods would mean bankruptcy. It was the case where the rich got richer just as the poor got poorer.

Believe it or not, it was at this very juncture that they decided to bail out these companies by also giving them money to help them survive. This was funny for this is the same government that believed in the idea of the survival of the fittest. It was soon found out that it was these few companies that actually, after refusing to bribe the government into giving them this money, lobbied them. They had hired middlemen to do this dirty part of the job and it immediately shied away from being bribery or pen robbery to lobbing. The money was soon given out and the individual chief executive officers got most of it as bonuses for attracting capital to their respective companies, while at the same time heading for greener pastures overseas.

Apart from these bonuses, two of them arranged to be fired. They each got a couple of millions from the bail out money as severance bonus. The masterstroke was that they simply exchanged jobs and received further sign on bonuses.

What the government did next was to increase minimum wage for its people and people were very happy with them. There was however a catch in this ill-advised move. As soon as the minimum wage went up by five percent, the rest followed suit, some by over twenty percent. The domino effect on prices was the main issue. Marketers of course had to increase the price of goods to take care of those increases and in no time at all prices had gone up by over twenty percent. Who was at the loosing end? It was the man who got the minimum wage. His earnings had gone up, but his purchasing power had gone disproportionately downwards.

In a panic, the government finally decided to cut down on expenditures. It started off by stopping the idea of going to space since there had not been any obvious benefits from such ventures except to make them look very powerful. It however started off the probe of far off space where no other had tried. For what purpose they did this no one was sure of except that it was to boost their ego.

As if this was not enough, they began to attack other villages. This was at a high cost to the village since it was very costly to wage a war. They even had to borrow money from other friendly villages to wage these wars. They then began to develop and test new military hardware and this worsened their economy but they were not concerned, as they remained happy in their failure.

It was mainly because of this development that the gods then decided to look into the wars that were beginning to proliferate.

THE GODS ARE NOT TO BLAME

The history of man is often more like the history of wars in which man is involved big and small. In some of them one village would just like to dominate another for economic gains, or just to show off her power. At times it could arise from border disputes and in some instances it could be from mere trifles like dispute over games as had been seen earlier on in the book.

Acadia had perfected the art of the manufacture of wars just as others have tried to perfect the art of the manufacture of consumables. One of the easiest reasons that they had given for this stance of belligerency was that they were not trying to build an empire but were only trying to police the world. Funny enough, the idea of policing happens to signify dominance since one can only police someone under his jurisdiction.

Democracy was invented and perfected by other countries, but Acadia had come to put a definite twist to it. Though the gods have never been democratic in any of their dealings, Acadia had come to claim that it was what the gods wanted.

Their own brand of democracy had nothing noteworthy to write home about, though they were all out to spread it. One of their presidents was claimed to have gone into office after winning ten million votes from the eight million registered voters. When his election was challenged in court, the learned judge upheld the result on the basis that the election was so democratically conducted that the voters enthusiastically went in to vote. Though there were only eight million registered voters, that situation made some two million other eligible and qualified voters to come in and vote. He did not see why they should disenfranchise voters their constitutional rights to vote.

That was democracy at its best. It was because of this problem that god did not want his chosen children to have a king in the beginning. According to the Christian bible, they requested for one and he simply chose one for them. There was no democratic consideration. After he gave them the second king, it began to run in the family. That was in direct contradistinction to the idea of democracy and so it was soon thrown to the dogs.

In the case of Acadia as we had seen earlier, they had become one nation under God who was excluded from ruling, though they were still under him. One of the political parties actually always prided themselves as being the party with the largest Christian support. The priests here always helped to get them elected into office, usually so that after they had gone in they might receive some money. Unfortunately, it is this same group that always pointed out that one could not serve both God and Mammon together.

Incidentally it so happens that it is this very party that always leads them into wars. It always struggles to bring the light of democracy to the infidels, democratic infidels that is. Villages were attacked and looted, leaders were deposed and at times assassinated while alliances, no matter how unholy they might be, were forged, as long as they were going to gain from such.

However, it is claimed that the taste of the cake, be it pudding, is in the eating. The gods knew the exact reasons behind those wars. First and foremost, they were launched in order to secure natural resources. It is not that they did not have those very same resources, but since man is an ever wanting animal, they just wanted some more. Funny enough, though they had the Christian coalition as their allies, none of them seemed to see this as a violation of that biblical commandment that one should not covert. It seemed to be a case of the blind leading those who are supposed to be able to see while even explaining to them the exact colors that they were looking at.

As they also noticed, at times wars were pure business ventures. To do this some of those who were higher up would front companies that worked for and with the army in the war fronts. One such company for instance catered for their meals. It billed the government about three times the normal retail value for the meals. To make matters worse it catered for about one and a half times the number of soldiers that were available there. In their own defense they claimed that the prices were outrageously high because of the risk of sending the food to the war front, and they provided more so that even if some fell into the hands of the enemy they would still have enough for their boys.

Another bizarre one was that there were civilian contractors who worked as security men to protect the soldiers and their goods. Nothing could be more bizarre than a civilian protecting a soldier around the war front. As crazy as it might sound, they even earned more that five times what the soldiers that they were protecting earned.

Of course there was another one. The defense industry had been privatized. These new owners manufactured and sent their new weapons to the front to be tested. This is therefore the group that sort of tends to cash in on mayhem and destruction. They would always precipitate wars so that they could sell their products or at least demonstrate their capabilities to potential buyers. Most of these defense contractors had one thing or the other to do with the rulers.

Funny enough in one particular instance, inferior body armors were supplied to the soldiers in the front by such a defense contractor. His prices were also prohibitingly higher than that of the rest that were better. Many soldiers died from this deal and to them, they died doing what they loved to do best, or maybe they died serving their country, which was the ultimate sacrifice to show their patriotism. The important thing is that these contractors at home have made their money, having been very patriotic to their individual pockets.

These last reports as well as all the other reports were filed away in the archives of the celestial library. The gods had decided that the best thing to do would be to leave man alone to follow his path to imminent destruction, which even they themselves know about and refer to it as Armageddon. They even agreed that they were nearing the end times.

Man was already moving very fast towards self-destruction, though they claim that God might do it for them. The gods had decided to leave man alone to follow this unenviable path because he had become totally disobedient when it came to obeying the survival laws that had been laid down for them. He had even gone further to often challenge God himself. There had even been many instances of individual humans getting up to declare themselves God.

They were aware of the fact that if man did not destroy the earth indirectly due to his recklessness, then he might do so directly. An example of their indirect tendencies is the issue of global warming. They are aware of the fact that it could lead to the destruction of life as we know it now on earth, but for political as well as economic reasons, they are not ready to take decisive action.

On the other hand, they had amassed so much weapons of mass destruction, as they called them, that they could very easily destroy the earth several times over in the twinkle of an eye. Thoughtlessly enough, they are still researching into more powerful ones. Isn't that a case of conscious madness? All they are waiting for is for a mentally unstable ruler to take over somewhere and unleash these weapons.

Man is therefore like some of the things that he had manufactured. They are each geared and rigged for self-destruction. This might be the reason for the recent interest in exploring the outer limits of the universe—to seek alternative homes after they have destroyed this one.

It is therefore obvious that no matter what happens; THE GODS ARE NOT TO BLAME, for whatever fate befalls man at the end.

GLOSSARY OF THE GODS

Acada: The god as well as patron saint of knowledge.

Achilles: A Greek mythological human with the blood of the gods and was a very

Good athlete.

Agaba-Idu: An evil-looking entertainer. He was debatably evil amongst the Ibos.

Agboghonmo: A middle aged pretty ancestral spirit for the Ibos

Agbonma: Twin sister to Agboghonmo and a niece twice removed from Aphrodite.

Ajambene: An Ibo demi-goddess and mother of Agaba-Idu and Mgbadike.

Ajondu: An Ibo demi-god and patron saint for those who leaved a reckless life.

Akalogoli: An Ibo demi-god and patron saint of the irresponsible characters.

Akawo:An Ibo god and patron saint of all secrateries. He is the grand secretary

General for all the other gods.

Akataka: A very youthful ancestral spirit amongst the Ibos,

Akwunachienyi: An entertainment minded Ibo demi-god.

Ani: The Ibo mother goddess who was in charge of fertility, taboos and justice.

Aphrodite: Greek goddess of love and she was a beautiful enchantress.

Ayaka: An Ibo evil god that had all magical powers.

Bacchus: Greek god of wine.

Banza: An indeterminate god of bazaars.

Chineke: Ibo for God the creator.

Eyo: A Yoruba ancestral spirit that was not too far removed from the Akataka,

God: The Supreme Being. Also a generic name for all the other gods.

Ifejioku: The demi-god that was in charge of new yam festivals.

Ijele: Ibo dancing mother god of beauty.

Iti: Ibo equivalent of Bacchus, the god of wine.

Itibolibo: A god and patron saint of imbeciles.

Itikili: Identical twin brother of Iti. He was in charge of over-fermented wine.

Jolly: The god of merriment.

Lucifer: Satan in his early days before his revolt against the God of goodness.

Medusa: The evil magician/demi-god that the Argonauts encountered.

Mercury: The Roman messenger god.

Muses: The nine female demi-goddesses that influenced meditation and poetry.

Ngbadike: The twin brother to Agaba-Idu.

Ogbazuluobodo: The spirit town crier who announces the arrival of Ayaka.

Ojionu: The Ibo ancestral spirit that talks a lot.

Okwonma: Another half—brother, or at times considered a cousin, to Agaba-Idu.

Osondu: The demi-god that makes people run for their lives.

Satan: The devil. Personifies everything that was bad.

Ulo: The Ibo god of playfulness.

Whocalledme: The mischievous god that is in charge of gossips.